umpy
Dog

HarperCollins *Children's Books*

It was a beautiful day in
Toy Town and Bumpy Dog
was feeling extra bouncy.
He bounced and bumped here
and there, sniffing the flowers
and chasing birds.

Then, a beautiful butterfly flew
past Bumpy Dog so he chased
it all the way down the street,
towards Noddy's House-for-One.

Meanwhile, Noddy was busy baking googleberry muffins in his House-for-One. Later that day, Clockwork Mouse was going to judge the Toy Town muffin baking competition.

"Mmm, delicious!" smiled Noddy as he tasted the mixture. "I hope these muffins are the tastiest Clockwork Mouse has ever tried!"

At last, Noddy's muffins were ready. He held the plate proudly as he started walking to the market where Dinah was collecting everybody's entries before the competition.

Noddy had not gone far before Bumpy Dog bounded up to him, still chasing the butterfly. Before Noddy could move –

Bump!

Bumpy Dog had knocked Noddy to the ground and the muffins had tumbled all over the street!

All of Noddy's muffins were ruined!
"You naughty, bouncy dog!" cried Noddy.
"Go away and don't come back
until you are feeling less bouncy!"

Noddy went back inside
to bake another batch
of googleberry muffins.
"I must hurry if I still want
to enter the competition,"
Noddy said to himself.

Poor Bumpy Dog walked off with his tail between his legs. He was feeling a little sorry for himself, but when he spotted Tessie Bear walking in the distance he cheered up.

Bump!

Bumpy Dog bounced around Tessie Bear so much that he nearly knocked her over, too! "Careful, Bumpy Dog!" said Tessie Bear, throwing a stick for him. "You're particularly bouncy today! Let's go for a walk before the muffin competition starts."

Bumpy Dog ran about in the countryside
fetching sticks that Tessie Bear threw
for him. Before long, they met Clockwork
Mouse, who was walking as fast
as his little legs would carry him.

"Hello, Tessie Bear! Hello, Bump-"
said Clockwork Mouse, but before
he could finish speaking, Bumpy Dog
had run off into the Dark Woods.

"Where is he going?" wondered Tessie Bear.

Tessie Bear and Clockwork Mouse followed Bumpy Dog into the Dark Woods, but they were not happy.

"The Dark Woods are so spooky!" cried Tessie. "I need to get back to Toy Town. Come out, Bumpy Dog!" called Clockwork Mouse.

But Bumpy Dog was following a trail and not listening. Clockwork Mouse caught up with him. "Look! Bumpy Dog has found a trail of muffin crumbs!"

Bumpy Dog and Clockwork Mouse started following the trail of crumbs through the Dark Woods. Tessie followed behind, but she was still scared.

Deeper into the woods they went until they spotted two figures moving in the distance. Crumbs seemed to be dropping from the plate they were carrying.

It was the Goblins!

The three friends watched the Goblins
take the muffins into their tree house
and come out again, empty-handed.

"What are the Goblins doing?"
whispered Tessie Bear.
"All the muffins in Toyland should
be at the baking competition
now, not in the Goblins' house!
I suspect Goblin mischief!"

Bumpy Dog sprang into action. He ran all
the way back into Toy Town before Tessie Bear
and Clockwork Mouse even noticed he'd gone.

Bumpy Dog saw Noddy delivering parcels
and bounced and bumped all around him.
Then he jumped into Noddy's car!

"Bumpy Dog! I see you're
just as bouncy as you were earlier!
What is the matter?" Noddy asked.
"Do you want me to take
you somewhere?"

Bumpy Dog barked as they arrived in the Dark Woods. He led Noddy to the Goblins' tree house where they found their friends. They all crept in and gasped as they saw the huge pile of muffins sitting in the middle of the room.

"The Goblins have stolen all of Toy Town's muffins!" cried Noddy.

Bumpy Dog's nose twitched and he ran out of the tree house again…

…and jumped right at the Goblins, knocking them off their feet!

The others ran out of the tree house when they heard the Goblins shouting.

"Right, you two," said Noddy. "We'll see what Mr Plod has to say about you stealing all of the muffins!"

Bumpy Dog helped Noddy put the Goblins in his car while Tessie Bear rescued the stolen muffins.

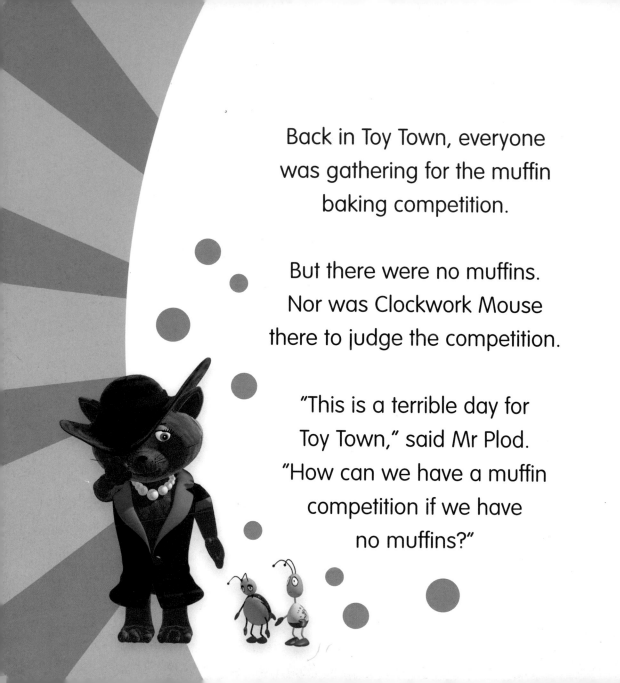

Back in Toy Town, everyone
was gathering for the muffin
baking competition.

But there were no muffins.
Nor was Clockwork Mouse
there to judge the competition.

"This is a terrible day for
Toy Town," said Mr Plod.
"How can we have a muffin
competition if we have
no muffins?"

"Parp-parp!" Just then, Noddy drove up with the Goblins and all the missing muffins. Clockwork Mouse, Tessie Bear and Bumpy Dog followed along behind.

"The Goblins had stolen all of our muffins but Bumpy Dog helped us catch the thieves!" called Noddy.

Mr Plod arrested the grumbling Goblins.

"Let the muffin competition begin!" cheered Clockwork Mouse.

"Here's to Bumpy Dog!"
cried Noddy, handing a bone
to his bounciest, bumpiest friend.
"Without him, the Goblins would
have eaten all our muffins!"

"*Woof Woof!*"
wagged Bumpy Dog.

First published in the UK by HarperCollins Children's Books in 2008

1 3 5 7 9 10 8 6 4 2

ISBN-13: 978-0-00-725899-4

ISBN-10: 0-00-725899-2

Printed and bound in China

NODDY™

Star in your very own PERSONALISED Noddy book!

In just 3 easy steps your child can join Noddy in a Toyland adventure!

1 Go to www.MyNoddyBook.co.uk

2 Personalise your book

3 Checkout!

3 Great Noddy adventures to choose from:

'Your child' Saves Toytown

Soar through a rainbow in Noddy's aeroplane to help him save Toytown.

A Gift for 'your child'

Noddy composes a song for your child in this story for a special occasion.

A Christmas Gift for 'your child'

Noddy composes a song for your child in a Christmas version of the above story.

Visit today to find out more and create your personalised Noddy book!

www.MyNODDYBook.co.uk